P9-APC-713

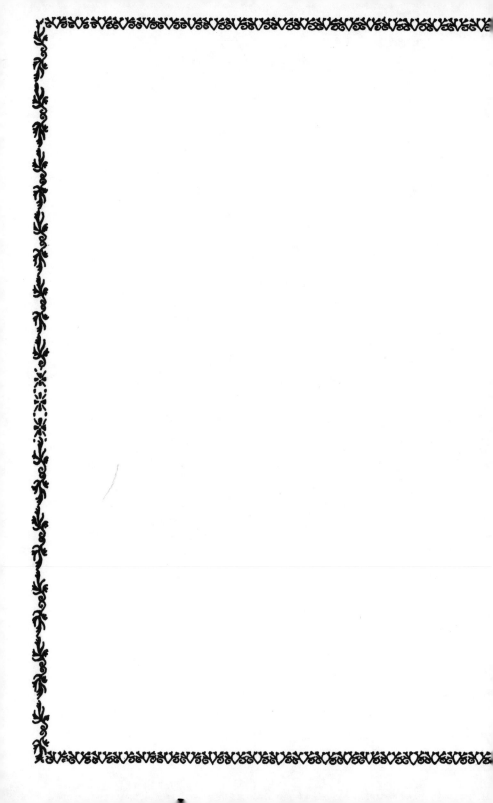

An I Can Read Book®

LITTLE BEAR

by
ELSE HOLMELUND MINARIK

pictures by MAURICE SENDAK

SCHOLASTIC INC.
New York   Toronto   London   Auckland   Sydney
Mexico City   New Delhi   Hong Kong   Buenos Aires

No part of this publication may be reproduced in whole or in part, or stored in a
retrieval system, or transmitted in any form or by any means, electronic, mechanical,
photocopying, recording, or otherwise, without the written permission of the publisher.
For information regarding permission, please write to HarperCollins Publishers,
10 East 53rd Street, New York, NY 10022.

I Can Read Book® is a registered trademark of HarperCollins Publishers Inc. All Rights Reserved.

Text copyright © 1957 by Else Holmelund Minarik.
Copyright © renewed 1985 by Else Holmelund Minarik.
Illustrations copyright © 1957 by Maurice Sendak.
Illustrations copyright © renewed 1985 by Maurice Sendak.
All rights reserved. Published by Scholastic Inc.,
557 Broadway, New York, NY 10012, by arrangement
with HarperCollins Publishers.
SCHOLASTIC and associated logos are trademarks and/or registered
trademarks of Scholastic Inc.

ISBN 0-439-45271-6

12 11 10 9 8 7 6 5 4 3 2 1   2 3 4 5 6 7/0

Printed in the U.S.A.

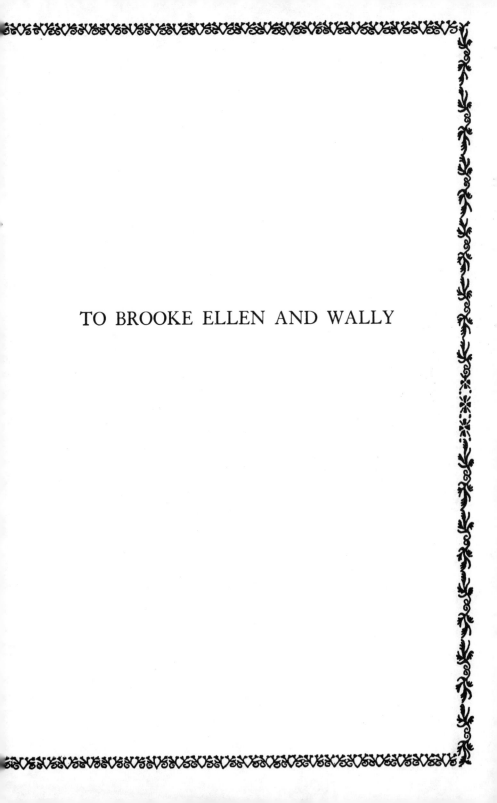

TO BROOKE ELLEN AND WALLY

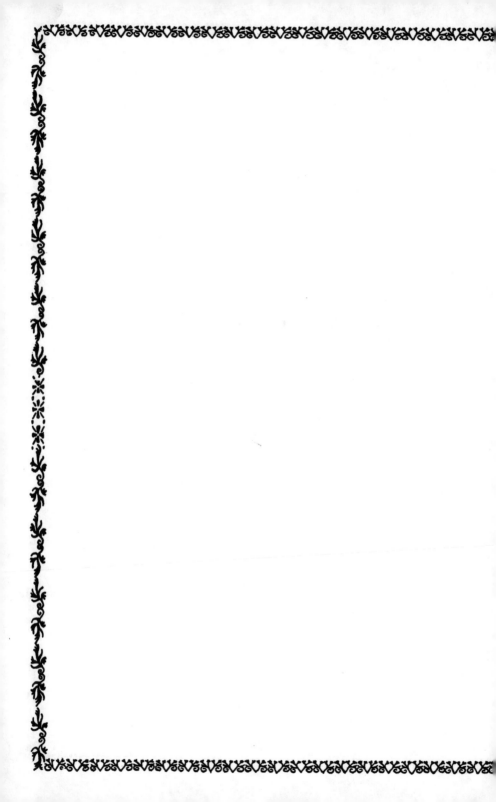

CONTENTS

What Will Little Bear Wear?   11

Birthday Soup   22

Little Bear Goes to the Moon   36

Little Bear's Wish   50

LITTLE BEAR

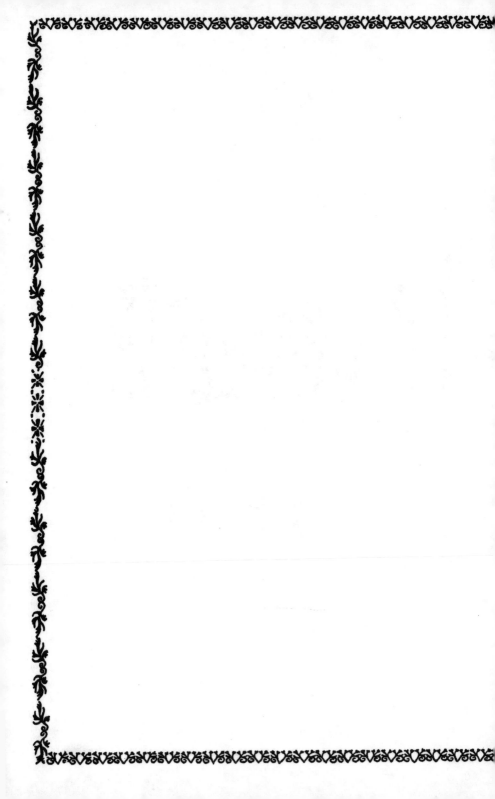

WHAT WILL LITTLE BEAR WEAR?

It is cold.

See the snow.

See the snow come down.

Little Bear said, "Mother Bear,

I am cold.

See the snow.

I want something to put on."

So Mother Bear made something

for Little Bear.

"See, Little Bear," she said,

"I have something for my little bear.

Here it is.

"Put it on your head."

"Oh," said Little Bear,

"it is a hat.

Hurray! Now I will not be cold."

Little Bear went out to play.

Here is Little Bear.

"Oh," said Mother Bear,

"do you want something?"

"I am cold," said Little Bear.

"I want something to put on."

So Mother Bear made something

for Little Bear.

14

"See, Little Bear," she said,

"I have something,

something for my little bear.

Put it on."

"Oh," said Little Bear,

"it is a coat.

Hurray! Now I will not be cold."

Little Bear went out to play.

Here is Little Bear again.

"Oh," said Mother Bear,

"do you want something?"

"I am cold," said Little Bear.

"I want something to put on."

So Mother Bear made something

again for Little Bear.

"See, Little Bear," she said,

"here is something,

something for my little bear.

Now you cannot be cold.

Put it on."

"Oh," said Little Bear,

"snow pants. Hurray!

Now I will not be cold."

Little Bear went out to play.

Here is Little Bear again.

"Oh," said Mother Bear,

"what can you want now?"

"I am cold," said Little Bear.

"I want something to put on."

"My little bear," said Mother Bear,

"you have a hat,

you have a coat,

you have snow pants.

Do you want a fur coat, too?"

"Yes," said Little Bear.

"I want a fur coat, too."

Mother Bear took the hat, the coat,

and the snow pants.

"See," said Mother Bear,

"there is the fur coat."

"Hurray!" said Little Bear.

"Here is my fur coat.

Now I will not be cold."

And he was not cold.

What do you think of that?

BIRTHDAY SOUP

"Mother Bear,

Mother Bear,

Where are you?" calls Little Bear.

"Oh, dear, Mother Bear is not here,

and today is my birthday.

"I think my friends will come,

but I do not see a birthday cake.

My goodness—no birthday cake.

What can I do?

The pot is by the fire.

The water in the pot is hot.

If I put something in the water,

I can make Birthday Soup.

All my friends like soup.

Let me see what we have.

We have carrots and potatoes,

peas and tomatoes;

I can make soup with

carrots, potatoes, peas and tomatoe

23

So Little Bear begins to make soup

in the big black pot.

First, Hen comes in.

"Happy Birthday, Little Bear," she says.

"Thank you, Hen," says Little Bear.

Hen says, "My! Something smells good here.

Is it in the big black pot?"

"Yes," says Little Bear,

"I am making Birthday Soup.

Will you stay and have some?"

"Oh, yes, thank you," says Hen.

And she sits down to wait.

Next, Duck comes in.

"Happy Birthday, Little Bear," says Duck.

"My, something smells good.

Is it in the big black pot?"

"Thank you, Duck," says Little Bear.

"Yes, I am making Birthday Soup.

Will you stay and have some with us?"

"Thank you, yes, thank you," says Duck.

And she sits down to wait.

Next, Cat comes in.

"Happy Birthday, Little Bear," he says.

"Thank you, Cat," says Little Bear.

"I hope you like Birthday Soup.

I am making Birthday Soup."

Cat says, "Can you really cook?

If you can really make it,

I will eat it."

"Good," says Little Bear.

"The Birthday Soup is hot,

so we must eat it now.

We cannot wait for Mother Bear.

I do not know where she is."

"Now, here is some soup for you, Hen,"

says Little Bear.

"And here is some soup for you, Duck,

"and here is some soup for you, Cat,

and here is some soup for me.

Now we can all have some Birthday Soup."

Cat sees Mother Bear at the door,

and says, "Wait, Little Bear.

Do not eat yet.

Shut your eyes, and say one, two, three."

Little Bear shuts his eyes

and says, "One, two, three."

Mother Bear comes in with a big cake.

"Now, look," says Cat.

"Oh, Mother Bear," says Little Bear,

"what a big beautiful Birthday Cake!

Birthday Soup is good to eat,

but not as good as Birthday Cake.

I am so happy you did not forget."

"Yes, Happy Birthday, Little Bear!"

says Mother Bear.

"This Birthday Cake is a surprise for you.

I never did forget your birthday,

and I never will."

LITTLE BEAR GOES TO THE MOON

"I have a new space helmet.

I am going to the moon," said Little Bear to

Mother Bear.

"How?" asked Mother Bear.

"I'm going to fly to the moon,"

said Little Bear.

"Fly!" said Mother Bear.

"You can't fly."

"Birds fly," said Little Bear.

"Oh, yes," said Mother Bear.

"Birds fly, but they don't fly to the moon.

And you are not a bird."

"Maybe some birds fly to the moon,

I don't know.

And maybe I can fly like a bird,"

said Little Bear.

"And maybe," said Mother Bear,

"you are a little fat bear cub

with no wings and no feathers.

"Maybe if you jump up
you will come down very fast,
with a big plop."

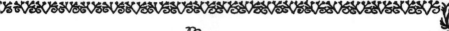

"Maybe," said Little Bear.
"But I'm going now.
Just look for me up in the sky."
"Be back for lunch," said Mother.

Little Bear thought.

I will jump from a good high spot,

far up into the sky,

and fly up, up, up.

I will be going too fast

to look at things,

so I will shut my eyes.

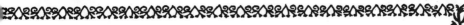

Little Bear climbed to the top of a little hill,

and climbed to the top of a little tree,

a very little tree on the little hill,

and shut his eyes and jumped.

Down, down he came with a big plop,

and down the hill he tumbled.

Then he sat up and looked around.

"My, my," he said.

"Here I am on the moon.

"The moon looks just like the earth.

Well, well," said Little Bear.

"The trees here look just like our trees.

The birds look just like our birds.

"And look at this," he said.

"Here is a house that looks just like my house.

I'll go in and see what kind of bears live here.

"Look at that," said Little Bear.

"Something to eat is on the table.

It looks like a good lunch for a little bear."

Mother Bear came in and said,

"But who is this?

Are you a bear from Earth?"

"Oh, yes, I am," said Little Bear.

"I climbed a little hill,

and jumped from a little tree,

and flew here, just like the birds."

"Well," said Mother Bear.

"My little bear did the same thing.

He put on his space helmet and flew to Earth.

So I guess you can have his lunch."

Little Bear put his arms around Mother Bear.

He said, "Mother Bear, stop fooling.

You are my Mother Bear

and I am your Little Bear,

and we are on Earth, and you know it.

Now may I eat my lunch?"

"Yes," said Mother Bear,

"and then you will have your nap.

For you are my little bear,

and I know it."

"Little Bear," said Mother Bear.

"Yes, Mother," said Little Bear.

"You are not asleep," said Mother Bear.

"No, Mother," said Little Bear.

"I can't sleep."

"Why not?" said Mother Bear.

"I'm wishing," said Little Bear.

"What are you wishing for?"
said Mother Bear.

"I wish that I could sit on a cloud
and fly all around," said Little Bear.
"You can't have that wish, my Little Bear,"
said Mother Bear.

"Then I wish that I could find a Viking boat,"

said Little Bear.

"And the Vikings would say,

'Come along, come along!

Here we go. Away! Away!'"

"You can't have that wish, my Little Bear,"

said Mother Bear.

"Then I wish I could find a tunnel,"
said Little Bear.

"Going all the way to China.
I would go to China and come back
with chopsticks for you."

"You can't have that wish, my Little Bear,"
said Mother Bear.

"Then I wish I had a big red car,"

said Little Bear.

"I would go fast, fast.

I would come to a big castle.

"A princess would come out and say,

'Have some cake, Little Bear,'

and I would have some."

"You can't have that wish, my Little Bear,"

said Mother Bear.

"Then I wish," said Little Bear,

"a Mother Bear

would come to me and say,

'Would you like to hear a story?' "

"Well," said Mother Bear,

"maybe you can have that wish.

That is just a little wish."

"Thank you, Mother," said Little Bear.

"That was what I really wanted

all the time."

"What kind of story would you

like to hear?" said Mother Bear.

"Tell me about me,"

said Little Bear.

"Tell me about things

I once did."

"Well," said Mother Bear,

"once you played in the snow,

and you wanted something to put on."

"Oh, yes, that was fun,"

said Little Bear.

"Tell me something more about me."

"Well," said Mother Bear,

"once you put on your space helmet

and played going to the moon."

"That was fun, too,"

said Little Bear.

"Tell me more about me."

"Well," said Mother Bear,

"once you thought you had no Birthday Cake,

so you made Birthday Soup."

"Oh, that was fun," said Little Bear.

"And then you came with the cake.

You always make me happy."

"And now," said Mother Bear,

"you can make me happy, too."

"How?" said Little Bear.

"You can go to sleep,"

said Mother Bear.

"Well, then, I will," said Little Bear.

"Good night, Mother dear."

"Good night, Little Bear.

Sleep well."

The End